OXFORD
UNIVERSITY PRESS

Great Clarendon Street, Oxford OX2 6DP

Oxford University Press is a department of the University of Oxford.
It furthers the University's objective of excellence in research, scholarship,
and education by publishing worldwide in

Oxford   New York

Auckland   Cape Town   Dar es Salaam   Hong Kong   Karachi
Kuala Lumpur   Madrid   Melbourne   Mexico City   Nairobi
New Delhi   Shanghai   Taipei   Toronto

With offices in

Argentina   Austria   Brazil   Chile   Czech Republic   France   Greece
Guatemala   Hungary   Italy   Japan   Poland   Portugal   Singapore
South Korea   Switzerland   Thailand   Turkey   Ukraine   Vietnam

Oxford is a registered trade mark of Oxford University Press
in the UK and in certain other countries

British Library Cataloguing in Publication Data

Data available

ISBN: 978-0-19-272499-1

5 7 9 10 8 6 4

Printed in Malaysia by Imago

Paper used in the production of this book is a natural,
recyclable product made from wood grown in sustainable forests.
The manufacturing process conforms to the environmental
regulations of the country of origin.

The THREE LITTLE PIGS

IAN BECK

OXFORD
UNIVERSITY PRESS

Once upon a time lived a mother pig, with her three little pigs. They lived happily together, but the mother pig was very poor, so she decided to send the three little pigs into the world to seek their fortunes.

They set off in the sunshine. Each carried his few treasures and some turnip tops for lunch. After a while, they reached a crossroads, and each little pig went down a different path.

The first little pig met a man carrying a
large bundle of straw.

'Excuse me,' he said, 'would you give me
some straw so that I may build a house?'

'Certainly,' said the man. 'It's making me
sneeze ...

achooo!'

The happy little pig built his house of straw,
and settled down to his new life.

Soon there was a knock at the door.

'Who's there?' asked the little pig.

'It's me … your friend … the wolf …
Won't you let me in?' said a growly voice.

'NO,' said the little pig. 'Not by the hair on
my chinny-chin-chin!' So the wolf said,

'Then I'll huff

and I'll puff

and I'll BLOW

your house down.'

And he huffed and he puffed, and down
fell the straw house. The poor little pig
ran off as fast as he could.

The second little pig had met a man who was carrying a bundle of sticks.

'Excuse me,' he asked, 'would you give me those sticks so I may build myself a house?'

'Of course,' replied the man. 'I've forgotten why I was carrying them in the first place.'

So the second little pig built himself a house. But soon there was a tap on the door.

'Who is it?' the little pig asked nervously.

'It's me. Your brother,' said a worried voice. 'Do let me in!'

The second little pig opened the door, and in fell his brother. He was out of breath, and just as he was about to speak, there came a loud knock at the door.

'Who's there?' asked the little pigs.

'It's me,' growled a sly voice. 'Open the door and let me in.'

'Never!' cried the two little pigs. 'Not by the hairs on our chinny-chin-chins, you shall never come in!'

So the wolf said,

'Then I'll huff

and I'll puff

and I'll BLOW

your house down.'

So he huffed and he puffed, and the house of sticks blew apart. The two little pigs ran off as fast as they could.

The third little pig had done exactly the same as his brothers. He had walked happily along the road and soon met a man who was pulling a cart laden with heavy bricks and bags of cement.

'Excuse me,' he asked, 'but might you spare me those bricks and some cement? They are just what I need to build a safe little house.'

'I'd be glad to,' said the man. 'Pulling this load is hard work.'

So the third little pig built his house. It had four square walls, and a fine chimney.

He had just settled down inside, when there came a tap at his door.

'Who's there?' he asked.

'It's us. Your brothers. *Please* let us in.'

The little pig opened his door, and in they tumbled. They were very out of breath. They had just started to speak when there came a loud knock on the door.

'Who's there?' said the little pigs.

'It's me,' said a gruff voice. 'Open the door and let me in!'

'Never!' cried the little pigs. 'Not by every hair on our chinny-chin-chins, you shall never come in.' So the wolf said,

'Then I'll huff
and I'll puff
and I'll BLOW
your house down…

and then I shall come in and eat you all up!'

The wolf drew in his breath.

He huffed, and he puffed. He puffed, and he huffed, until he could blow no more. But the little house stood firm.

The wolf was worn out. He was hungry and cross.

'I shall find another way in,' he snarled.

He began to climb on to the roof.

'He's going to come down the chimney,' said the first little pig.

'What shall we do?' said the second little pig.

'I know,' said the third little pig. 'We must build a fire.'

They set to, and soon had a good fire blazing.

The wolf lowered himself down the chimney. As his bottom inched downwards, so the flames inched upwards ... until suddenly ...

'YOWL!'

The wolf's bottom and tail were scorched and he shot out of the chimney sparking like a rocket.

The three little
pigs were never
troubled by the wolf
again. They lived happily in
the little brick house. Soon they
sent for their mother, and they
all lived happily together
for as long as they could.
Which was a very
long time.

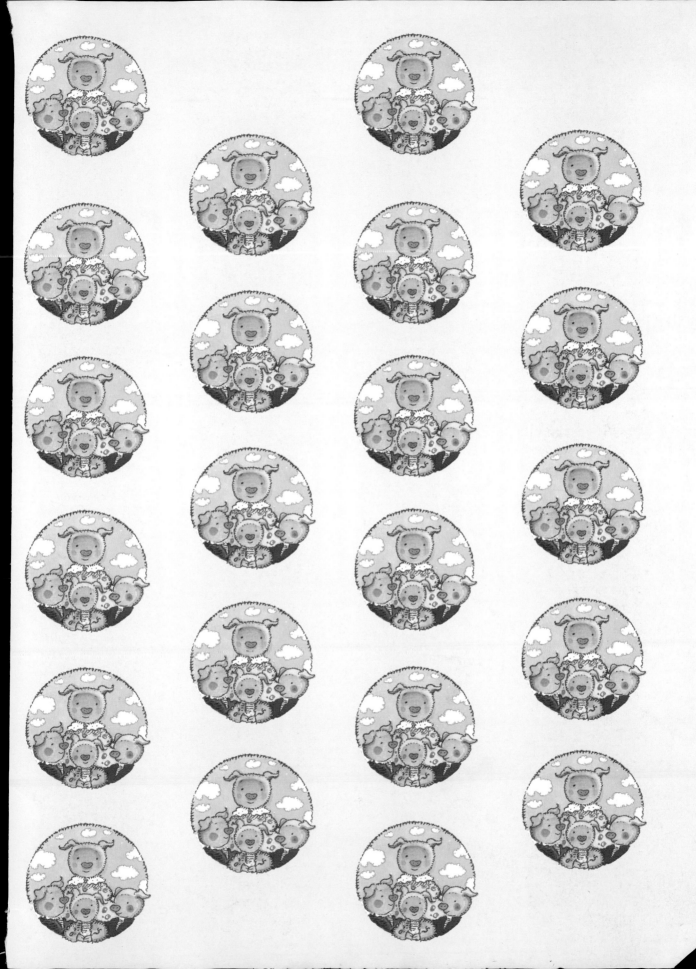